A Graphic Novel By Tim Mulligan

Illustrations by Pyrink

Snitchland: the Graphic Novel

This edition published by Highpoint Lit

For information, write to info@highpointpubs.com.

First Edition
ISBN: 979-8-9908488-0-1

Library of Congress Cataloging-in-Publication Data
Mulligan, Tim

Snitchland

Summary: "The story of Snitchland is based on hundreds of stories of whistleblowers in Richland – a small town in Eastern Washington State – deemed "the most toxic place in the Western Hemisphere. A ghost story, moving family drama, and cautionary tale about what can happen when people try to shed light on a dangerous aspect of one's community – and evil happens." —Provided by publisher.

ISBN: 979-8-9908488-0-1 (paperback)

1. Horror 2. Suspense

Library of Congress Control Number: 2024918967
Cover and Interior Design by Pyrink
Project Management by Steisha Ponczoch
Manufactured in the United States of America

Chapter ONE

Welcome to Hanford
WHERE SAFETY COMES FIRST

Hey everyone... Oh, hi!

Thanks so much for coming today. I really mean it. You all look great.

I know funerals are not for everyone – I personally am not a fan –
but I didn't have the choice not to attend this one.

I guess you could say I was... coaxed into attending. Unwillingly of course.

Richland.
Witchland.
Snitchland. This town.

I know most of you are from here. Probably even born here. Or moved here – like I did – to work, out there –

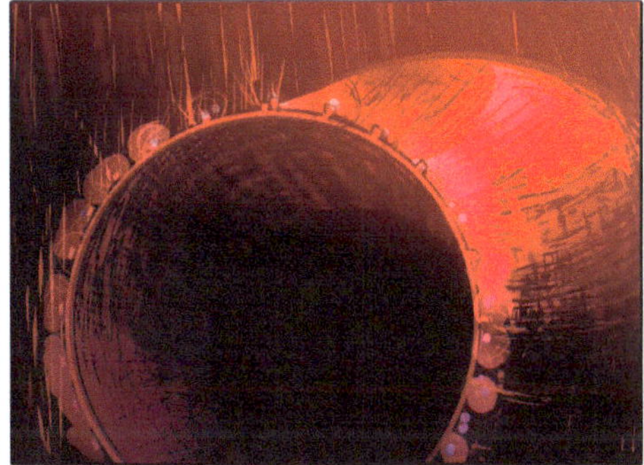

To Hanford. The bread and butter of this town. Of this entire part of the state. The livelihood of most of you.

But I see you.

I know that many of you are sick. Don't feel well.
Have health issues that you can't explain.

Or, you have parents, or relatives, or neighbors, who died here. Or are just sick – really fucking sick.
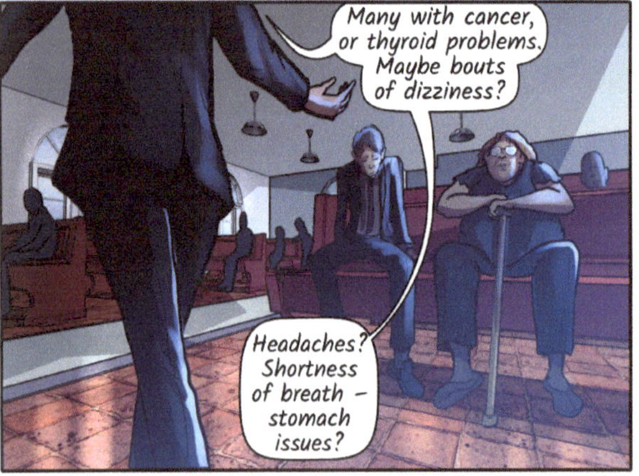
Many with cancer, or thyroid problems. Maybe bouts of dizziness?
Headaches? Shortness of breath – stomach issues?

Maybe can't get it up?
Metallic taste in your mouth?

You all know what's going on here – toxic vapors in the wind... breathing the dust, the air...
...swimming in that water. And I feel for you. I do.

Ali, Van, I am so sorry.
I brought you here, to this place.
Against your wishes. I didn't listen to your concerns. I should have. Van –

We never should have come here. You are the sweetest, most loving husband and father in the world – and I brought you here –
– thinking I was doing the right thing, new job, new experiences. I wanted to get us out of the mess of the past few years in Seattle –
but it turned into this terrible and awful chapter of our life.

Ali. You brought so much joy to my life, to Van's life, to everyone's life. And will continue to do so.

I'm so proud of you, and know you will conquer this world, be a real trail blazer.

But please, get out of here – out of this town – do great things. Just not here.

We shouldn't be here.
None of this should have happened.
But it did.

Some will say it's because there's evil in this town –
witchcraft, haunted sticks, ghosts.

Others will just blame it on the human body –
another "random" case of lung cancer – but I know the real murderer here –

And I think all of you know it as well. This has to stop. All of you can help make it stop.
There are too many of us here, like me, with me now...

...who want to see an end to this. Please, do the right thing and make it stop.

Thank you to our choir.
That was a lovely hymn.

Ladies and Gentlemen, on this sad day, we are honoring the life of a cherished member of our community,
Jared Fleming.

It's time to hear from those who knew and loved him the most – his family.

I'd like to invite Jared's husband, Van Fleming, to the podium to address you all.

I would like to thank you all for coming today.

Jared was full of – love, and goodness. Everyone loved Jared. I –

I loved him so much.
And though this town –

failed him in so many ways – he would be so moved to see you all here...

Well God dammit...

I am so sorry.
Shit. Look. Jared was the love of my life.
I don't know where I'd be without him.

Thank you Jared – for everything – you are – were – a beautiful man.
And an amazing dad to Ali...

Hi. I'm Ali. Jared is – was – my dad. My pops.
He was the glue that held us together. While my dad here – Van –
is the energy driving our house, Pops was the – stable one –

sorry Dad – but he kept us on track.

He brought us to this town – if I can steal his favorite phrase – as "Trail Blazers" - and we blazed through life with him leading us.

But none of this seems right. Everyone here – and out there – knows what really happened.

It wasn't just another random case of "the cancer." What happened to him – out there – is not okay.

Someone needs to stand up and take responsibility for what happened.
Hanford is not safe. Too many people have died, or gotten sick.

And for this to have happened to the sweetest man to ever walk this earth is a fucking crime.
Excuse my language. But it's not right.

Dad – I love you. I am so sorry the love of your life is gone.
I'm here for you, and always will be.

Pops – I will never stop thinking of you, of all the advice you've given me. I'm so sorry this happened to you. I love you so much.

At this time, while Jared's favorite songs play, I invite you to come up and say your farewells to Jared.
Then please join us in the lobby, and outside, for a small reception. Thank you all for coming and God bless.

Van, I'm so sorry for your loss. My name is... Jane.
I worked with Jared. On his team. Can we talk privately?

I just want to let you know what you probably already know – this was no random case of the cancer.
I was in the field that day. I know – for a fact – that this never should have happened.

The accident could have been completely avoided. That tunnel was not safe.
I reported it several times to management, including just a few days prior to the collapse.

I reported cracks, that kept growing.
But they ignored me, and then later told me I was wrong, like I was crazy or something.

If they had listened, this never would have happened.

What? Those fuckers! Jesus Christ...

Look, I'm sorry for laying this on you now. I was just so moved by this service. I felt I couldn't hold back.

But listen – they'll make my life hell – fire me, harass me – if they know we're speaking.
Whatever you do, please leave my name out of it.

Chapter TWO

Dad, I don't want to leave you here. I can contact the school, take a few more weeks off.
Or maybe I can skip this semester altogether. This is too much for you.

No way Ali.

You need to get back to school.
I'll be fine. It's what he would have wanted.
You have an amazing scholarship, and are crushing it, and you only have a few weeks left in the school year.

I'll see you in a few weeks, when school gets out.

We haven't even really talked about your plans.
Are you going to stay here? Or move back to Seattle? You hate it here.

I don't know yet. I'll probably move back, someday.
But for now... I still have my job at the restaurant, if you can call it that.
And we love this house.

Let's wait and decide all that later. Maybe when you're here this summer.

Really? You could sell this house now, make a good profit, and buy a house in Seattle, a town you love.

What? I know you – you've been holding back since the funeral.
What's going on with you?

Okay...but after I tell you this, you have to promise me you will still head back to school this week and finish the year.

Jesus Dad, what is it?
Do you promise me first?
Yes, Dad, I promise. Now what is it?

Something strange happened at the funeral. I'm still trying to process it.
At the end, before the reception, a woman came up to me – a little slip of a thang, dark glasses, really nervous-like.

She pulled me aside. I had no idea who she was so I obliged.
She told me her name was Jane, and that she worked with Jared out at Hanford. She said she was there that day.

I never heard Pops mention someone named Jane.

I'm pretty certain her name is not Jane. And besides, Jared kept all that work stuff to himself.
Anyway, she said she had complained about that tunnel not being safe more than once, even just before it collapsed.
She thought something like that might happen.
And that her bosses ignored her complaints and did nothing.

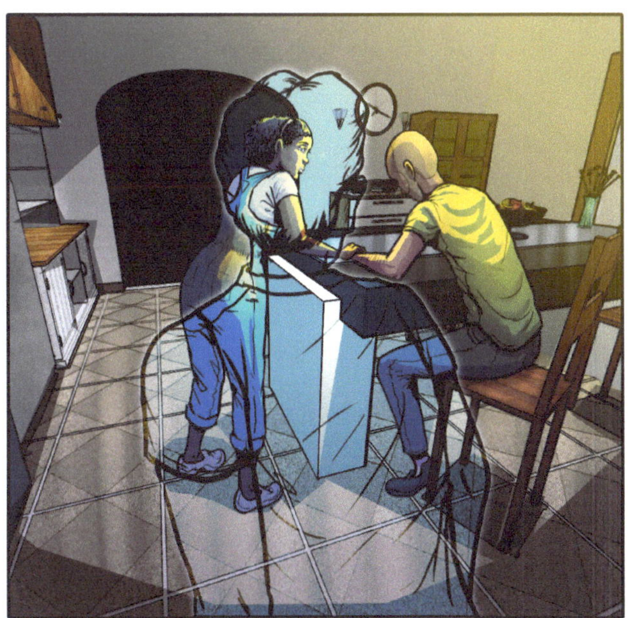

God dammit! No fucking way!

I just keep thinking about all he had to go through this past year – the radiation, the constant poking and prodding...

They even have the fucking balls to deny any liability, not even pay his medical bills –
...and they could have prevented this whole thing from happening in the first place.

Nothing about this is right. That must be illegal. We have to talk to someone, a lawyer. And bring "Jane" with us.

Jane is not Jane. And Not Jane is not helping.
She is terrified about them knowing she spoke to me – and like retaliating or something.

I don't know how to find her even if I wanted to.
Jared hardly talked about his co-workers.
Dad... it's Richland. Not New York City, or Seattle. I can find her.

I have a few days still. Let me think about this. We can't just let this go.

Dad - Do you feel him in the room with us?
I swear it feels like he's there, everywhere I go.

Oh thank God it's not just me. Girl, since he died, I feel him near me all the time.

I think sometimes he touches me, and sometimes when I'm sleeping, I can hear him whispering to me.

He would want this.
He would want us to find out what really happened, and maybe prevent this from happening to others.

Jesus fuck!
CRASH

He hated that vase.

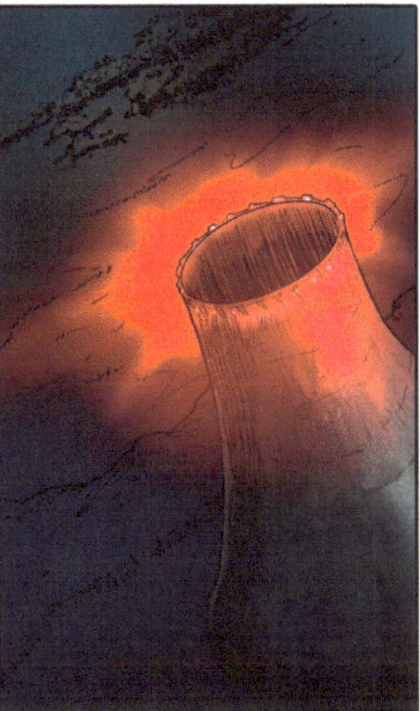

Welcome to Hanford
WHERE SAFETY COMES FIRST
Chapter THREE

I don't want to go back to school. It just sucks we have to go back, now.
I just want to stay here with you.

That's cray cray talk Shannon. Of course you have to go back. Finals are a few weeks away. I'm going back too.
I have to, even though I hate to leave my Dad here alone.

Well, I'll be here. Old Reliable Brett is going – um – nowhere.
I can check on him. Make sure he's okay.

That would be amazing Brett – you're the best.
And there's nothing wrong with staying and going to community college.
And he loves you too. With all we've –

...you've – gone through over the past year.
I really appreciate everything you guys have done to help us through this.

I can't believe he's gone. I mean, I know he was really sick... and went through so much... but I just can't believe he's really gone.

So Shannon... I have to ask... how are you doing?
All the nightmares and problems from last year – are they behind you now?

Ali, don't worry about me. I'm okay. I'm more worried about you now.
Especially since that old Witch died, it's definitely all behind us now.

Sad she died, but so glad we got through all that.
Well at least, we almost all did...

I have to tell you guys about something weird that happened at the funeral.

What?
What weird thing happened at the funeral?
Not sure I want to hear this...

Some mysterious lady pulled my Dad aside, and said she worked with Pops. At Hanford.

She said she'd known for a while that the tunnel was not safe –
there were cracks – and that she had reported it to management – more than once.
They told her she was wrong and ignored her complaints.

God dammit... this place is so fucked up!

We should talk to her - did she leave her name or phone number?

No - she said her name was "Jane." Dad is certain that's not her real name.
He said she seemed really nervous and didn't want to give any more info than that.

You know she's not the only one, right?

What are you talking about?
Brett...

What? What do you guys know that you aren't telling me?

You know I worked out there last summer? So did Shannon. We hear the whispers.
Apparently there are like literally hundreds of people – they call them whistleblowers –
They also call them snitches.

– okay, snitches. Who've made complaints over the years, even decades.
Or filed claims, even like lawsuits, about safety issues out there.

What?
You're kidding.

Uh, no, not kidding. You can look it up online –
it's no secret. But people out there...

...are scared to speak up. They say that bad shit happens to you if you voice any concerns, or make any complaints.
What kind of bad shit?

Come on Shannon, we've got to tell her.

God dammit you guys, tell me what? My Pops was just buried yesterday. Tell me what?

My uncle.
He was one.
A whistleblower.
He got sick out there – he worked at the tank farms.

Excuse me – what?

Tank farms.
There are like millions of gallons of toxic sludge buried in huge tanks under the ground.
In tanks.
Tank farms.

And they're leaking.

Leaking – into the ground? Why does no one talk about it?
You'd think that maybe we'd have learned something like this in school – oh, I don't know, since our fucking school sits within a mile of Hanford – and some fucking toxic leaking tank farms?

Look around, Ali.

Everyone works out there. It's why they live here – good pay, beautiful town, great place to raise kids...

...so no one wants to talk about it. Shannon, what happened to your uncle?

He got sick. The fumes and dust made him really sick. He couldn't even work anymore.
He complained about it to his managers and they denied any problems. He had to file a lawsuit.

Then all hell broke loose. Everyone called him a fucking snitch.

He was followed like everywhere he went.

Heard weird tapping and clicking on his phone – they were listening to him.
click
click
click
BZZZZ

And then his house was broken into, like, a few times.

Like they were sending him a message – a warning – to back down, or trying to find any evidence of his reports or whatever...

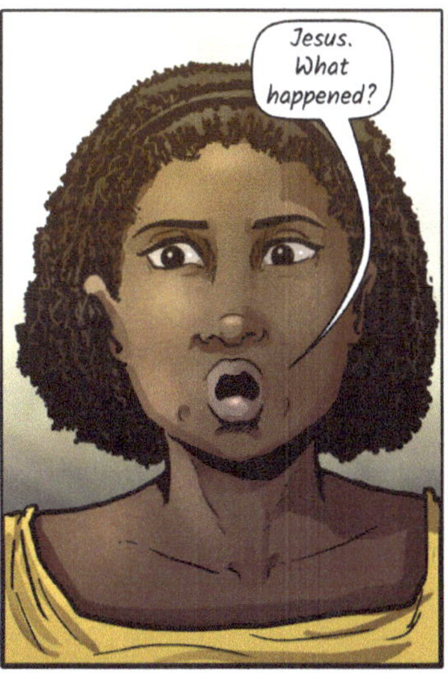
Jesus. What happened?

He found some group – out of Seattle – all made up of whistleblowers.
And people who either got sick or made complaints about safety issues out there. Like Brett said, apparently it's a huge network.

He claims they saved him. Helped him settle his claim. And got them to leave him alone.
Where is he now? Is he okay?

Well... no, he's not okay. He died a few years ago.

But I still feel his presence a lot –
he was my favorite uncle. I miss him so much.

I'm so sorry Shannon.
What is the name of that group from Seattle?
I don't remember exactly. Hanford something...

Click Click Click Click Click Click Click Click Click Click
Hanford Connect?
Click Click Click

Yes! Hanford Connect.
Ali, you need to be careful with this.

Thanks. I will – you know I'm always careful.
Hanford Connect. Look! They have a meeting here this week!

Welcome
Hanford
Connect
Chapter FOUR

Welcome
Hanford Connect

Welcome
Hanford Connect

Welcome
Hanford Connect

Welcome
Hanford Connect

Hey everyone – welcome welcome! This is –
Jesus, what is this – our April meeting of Hanford Connect.

I see many of our regulars – welcome back!
It looks like we have some newbies here as well.
Welcome! We'll do some intros in a little bit.

As a reminder for those of you who are new – all are welcome here!
Our goal here at Hanford Connect is to provide unique services for Hanford workers, current or former, who are ill or injured...
...along with employees who have raised concerns and are suffering reprisals. We are here for you, and are pleased –

well actually, kind of horrified to be honest – to say that we have now surpassed a milestone –

over 500 whistleblowers have come to us, to these meetings, to our office, or to secret meeting spots – since we came into existence a few decades ago.

First off, old business. I'm happy to say we've settled a few claims recently with some of our Hanford Connect whistleblowing family.
Welcome
Hanford Connect

Of course I can't divulge all the details – or deets as my granddaughter likes to say – of said settlements –

– but it is just good to know that we were able to help find some resolution for a few of you.

CLAP
CLAP
CLAP
CLAP
CLAP
CLAP
CLAP
CLAP
CLAP

What I can say is that two of these cases we've been working for several years -
no surprise, they have to do with the beryllium cases - or as we like to call them, our toxic dust problem.

I know we have one of the claimants here tonight. I won't say a name - but I will pause for a second. If you choose to stand up, and tell your story, please feel free. Absolutely no pressure.

Thanks George. I don't mind.

It's no secret about that dust - and this story should be told.
My name's Karen.

My son Jake started working out at Hanford back in 2006. He was only 22. He worked at the tank farms - in the thick of it.
After about a year, he started getting sick. Real sick. He was having trouble breathing - getting real real dizzy. His co-worker had the same problems.
Jake went to several doctors - they couldn't figure it out - but after a bunch of testing, they told him that he had beryllium in his lungs. And it had to have come from the dust out there. It had to have.

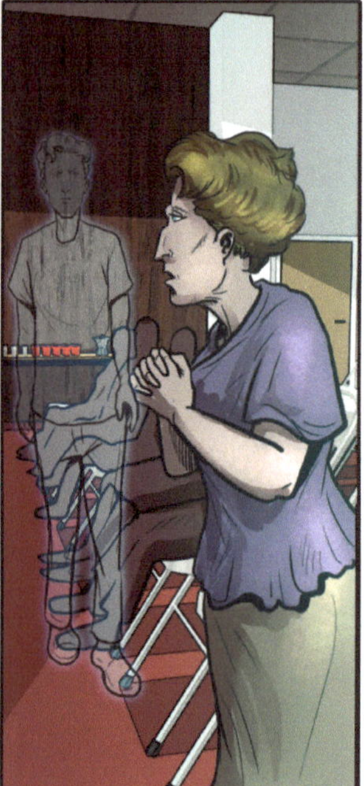

Of course he told his managers. Several times. They didn't care – didn't take him seriously, didn't believe him.
When he kept getting sicker, he took it to Human Resources – if you can really even call them that – and filed a formal report. A Workers Comp claim. Of course they denied it.

It was right after that that a bunch of weird stuff started to happen.
We'd see a van in front of our house, almost every night.

We'd hear weird noises and breathing on our house phone. We all knew someone was listening. That lasted for weeks.

Then he got worse. He developed the cancer – you know we all just call it "the cancer" around here, but everyone is afraid to talk about it.

Even with all that happening, they had the nerve to send him to a psychologist – like it wasn't happening, like he was crazy.

The official cause of his death was something called "chronic beryllium disease" – I just call it the cancer.

But yes, he fucking died. At 26 years old. Please excuse my French.

Thanks to George - and his sticking by my family for years and years of bullshit depositions and lawsuits - we finally have put this to rest. Of course, they aren't admitting anything.
Fucking assholes. Excuse my French again. God, I swear all the time now. I never used to.

But I have to admit, the money settlement is a huge help. It won't bring my Jakie back - but it can certainly help us to move on.

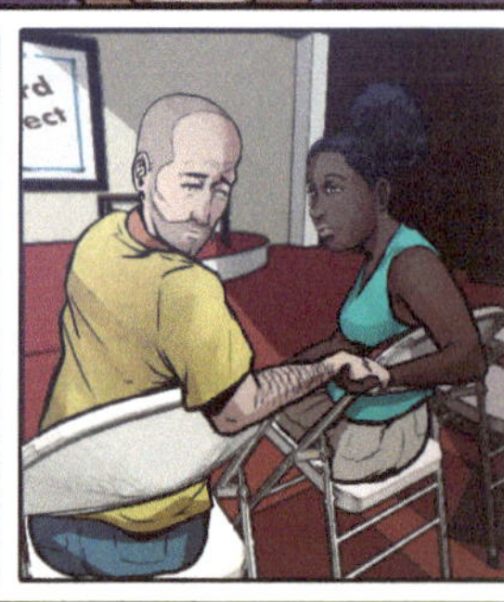

You all just need to keep up the fight. Don't give up. Don't let them win.
They are spending millions - billions - out there for this clean-up that's going fucking nowhere...

CLAP
CLAP
CLAP
CLAP
CLAP
CLAP
CLAP
CLAP
CLAP
CLAP
CLAP

Welcome
Hanford Connect

CLICK

CLICK

CLACK

CLICK

CLICK
CLACK

Sorry about that. This place seems to have electrical issues –
though they seem to happen mostly at these meetings!

Karen, thanks so much for sharing your story –
it's been a pleasure getting to know you and your family, and helping to bring some closure for at least one family.

Look, I'm glad for you ma'am – and so sorry for what you have had to endure – but this shit keeps happening!

It's not just the Downwinders, and what they endured.
I know everyone in town is afraid to talk about this, this horseshit, but God dammit someone has to!

It is happening to our friends and family every day, and no one will talk about it.

You all know that my son died five years ago – and I know many others in this town – in this room – who've gone through the same – yet no one talks about it!
They are afraid of getting fired...or having their homes broken into, or followed, or all of those other things we have heard about for years.
Hell, I'd bet that they are in this room, spying on all of us, all of this.

Brother Larry – we feel your pain. We do. And since you mentioned recent cases, let's just jump into it. We have a few new matters to speak of.
First, we have been getting reports from at least a dozen workers at the tank farms of recent strange odors – they'd been digging out there a bunch recently – and from what I can reckon, nearly twelve of them went to the hospital, and three are still there, as of today.

We are getting to the bottom of this, and working with the Department of Energy to stop that work immediately.

Also, you all heard about the tunnel that collapsed out there last year.
There is talk that at least one employee made complaints about cracks in the tunnel, several times, and all went ignored.

I think they even tried to patch them up with some shitty grout or something ineffective like that. You know the rest of the story.

And just recently, one of the workers who was there that day, working in that same tunnel – our brother and colleague Jared Fleming – has passed away, from lung cancer contracted not long after the tunnel collapse.

I would like us to give a warm Hanford Connect welcome to his husband Van, and his daughter Ali, who are here tonight. Ali, Van, we are so sorry for your loss. Do you want to say anything to the group?

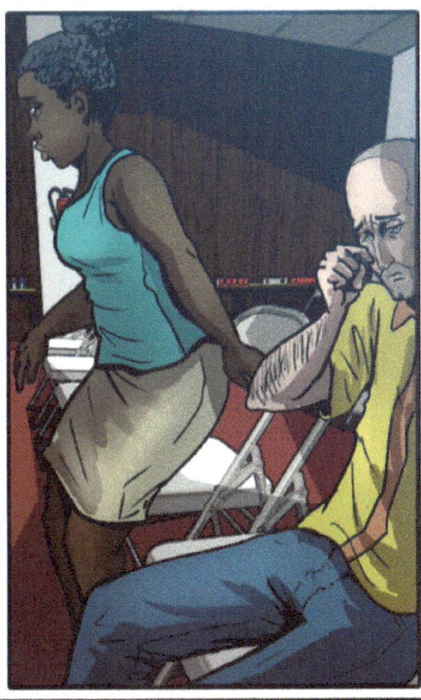

Hi. My dad and I are so moved by these stories. By all of you. We had no idea that this was happening – that you all existed – that these stories existed. I mean, we knew all about the Downwinders...

I feel him around me all the time. I don't know if it's the same for you – Karen – and you –

Larry. His name's Larry.

...Larry. But I know my Pops is here with us, and we need to do the right thing here.
He should not have died. That could have been avoided.

Someone working out there complained about it, and nothing was done about it.
And now I've lost a parent... and he -

He has lost a husband. The love of his life.
I've tried to get help - I've gone to the offices there, but you can't talk to a live person, let alone get past security.

I've tried to do my own investigating, and reach out to his co-workers - but no one will talk to me. To us.
If any of you can help me out - help us out - with any info about what really happened with that tunnel - what complaints were made about it.

Anything. Please let me know.
I thank you so much in advance, and am so happy I've found you all.

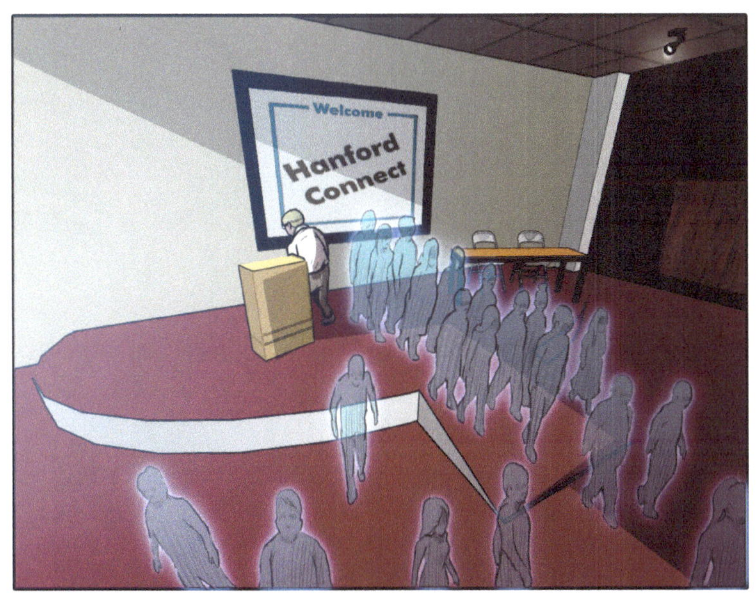
Welcome
Hanford Connect

Ali, Van, thank you so much for coming here tonight.
I give you my word that we are here to help. Let's talk this week about next steps.

And to you all out there – if you know of anyone who may have complained about the tunnel, or was working with Jared Fleming out there, please let me know.

Because as Ali said, one of the hardest parts with all of this is getting people to talk, and come forward. Because we all know the risks that come with that.

I look forward to seeing you all at our next meeting, next month.
Until then, keep up the good work, and the good fight. Be strong. Be vigilant.

Welcome to Hanford
WHERE SAFETY COMES FIRST
Chapter FIVE

CLINCK
CLINCK
CLINCK
CLINCK

RING
RING

Hello?
Oh hi Mom.
What - Oh -
TGIF to you
as well.

Though what makes this Friday more special than any other day of the week? Huh? Sorry, I've had a rough day today.

No, I promise I'm staying sober. Ali would kill me if I started drinking again.
TICK

No, Ali has not gone back to school yet. She's staying here with me a few more days. Then I'm forcing her to go back.
She's so close to finals – I don't want her to throw it all away after she's worked so hard this semester.

This summer? Not sure yet. She wants us to move, get out of this godforsaken town. But I'm not quite ready yet.

I feel like I need to just see a few more things through.

Yes, I still manage the donut place – it's called the Spudnut Shack. I've taken the past few weeks off, but I need to get back.

Them crullers are a'callin. Cruller, mom. It's a crispy fried donut. Like you haven't had your share of crullers in your life. Oh for fuck's sake, you have so.
The Spudnut Shack

What? Oh, just some things. I need to go through all of Jared's things. And tie up a few loose ends with his work.

Mom, did you hear that? Those clicks?
I keep hearing weird clicking noises every time I'm on the phone.
You didn't hear that?

What loose ends? Oh, it's complicated. I'll tell you about it later.

Yes, I promise to stay away from alcohol. That's the last thing any of us need.

CRASH

Jesus fuck!

What? Sorry mom to scream in your ear. Things are weird around here these days.
What? No, don't come visit. I can manage.

The last thing we need is for you to come and get "the cancer," at your age. Me? Mommie Dearest, I'm still young. Okay, younger than you, but still youngish.

What? Don't you dare call me a senior citizen. How dare you.

Wait – can you hear that again – that tapping? Is someone else on this call? Mom, don't you hear that?
Look, I should go. Let's talk soon. Bye mom.

Hello? Anybody there? Who is this?

Jared, is that you? Are you there?

Look, I know someone is here, in this room, now, with me – other than me.
And I know this town is haunted – but for fuck's sake, Jared – if that's you – you have to let me know.

I can't even fathom being terrorized by some random nuclear toxic demon or ghost here.
Please let it be you.

BEEP

That's our wedding song. How the hell...

Holy shit. I knew it was you...

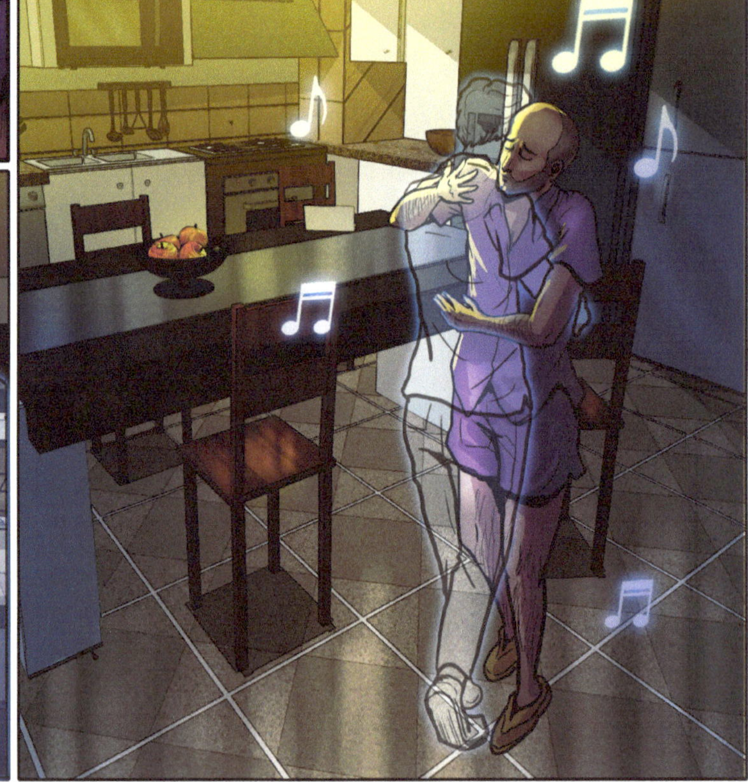

My God. Are we really dancing? To our wedding song? Oh my God I'm Demi Moore.
This can't be happening.

Jared, I love you so much. I miss you so much. I don't know how I'm going to go on without you...

Dad, everything okay here?

BEEP

Sorry to interrupt. Looks like you're having a moment.

It's okay honey – I seem to be having moments now every moment of every day. But I'm okay...
What happened here?

Oh, a glass of ice tipped over. No biggie.

How are you doing today? Have you left the house at all?
It's been a rough day.

Lots of thoughts in my head about Jared, about "Jane," and all of this.
And of course, I can't stop thinking about that meeting yesterday, and those poor people and their tragic stories.

I'm right there with you. It was maddening. And it's so clear now that we need to find out who this "Jane" really is. I can't believe Pops never introduced us to any of his coworkers.
Are you sure you haven't seen her at the Spudnut Shack? I thought the whole town hangs out there.

Honey, I haven't been back to that grease pit since the week before the funeral.

Dad... I have to ask you something. And I don't want you to think I'm crazy.
Ali, nothing would make me think you're crazy. You are the sanest person I know.

Do you feel him here in this room – with us now?

Him?
Jared?
Yes – Pops. I keep sensing him near me wherever I go. And sometimes I can feel him touch my shoulder, or brush up against me.
I think I can even hear him whispering things to me sometimes. And I'm pretty sure he's with us right now.

Oh thank you Jesus. I thought it was just me. And I'm not even drinking anymore.

Ali girl, he's everywhere. He is here now – we were just dancing!

He pushed that glass over. I think maybe it was a sign that he wants me to stay sober.
With what we went through last year with Judith, and all that witchcraft shit here in Witchland, nothing would surprise me. I hope it's true – I hope he's here with us.
Pops, if you are here – please, stay with us, always. We love you so much.
And we want so bad to help settle this mess with Hanford – none of you should have been working out there, and they know it.

Especially little "Jane" – Jared, who is Jane? We need to find her.

Pops, I have no idea what you are able to do, and how you can communicate with us. But if there is a way...

Honey, if Little Baby Ali here can create a magic salt circle to ward off witches, then there must be some way you can communicate with us...

CLICK

CLACK
Dad! Look!

Ali, that's a game cabinet.
All of our games are in there. Maybe it's a sign he misses our Farkle nights?

Ummm, Dad...

Oh, shit.

OUIJA

Chapter SIX

Fuck.
Ding-Dong
Shit.

Okay Dad, here we go. Remember, don't freak them out. Let me do the explaining.

Are you sure I can't have one drink? Just a nip?
If ever there was a time to start drinking again, this would be that time.
Don't even think about it.

Hey guys! Thanks for coming!

Hey you two lovebirds. Thanks for coming over.
We wanted to get a chance to say goodbye to you Shannon, before you head back this week. I'm leaving in a few days too.

Of course, thanks for having us over.
Van, we haven't seen you since – the funeral – and of course you've been on our minds.
How are you doing?

Oh you know... I'm getting by. Luckily Ali's been here to keep me company. And keep me sober.

Van, Ali, I know we've said this a bunch – but Shannon and I are so so sorry about what happened to Jared. It blows.
And I want you to know, Van, how inspiring it was to see how well you took care of him over the past few months.

You're an amazing person... and I know Jared felt the same. And after Ali and Shannon leave this week, know that I'm here, and you can call me anytime.

Thanks, both of you. Let's just try to move forward. And have a good night tonight. We ordered pizza from Atomic Pizza!
We ordered the Plutonium Pepperoni and Bombastic Veggie –

Ali... what's this for?
Oh – that – let me explain.

A Ouija Board? That's what this pizza party is about?
Ali, there's no way I'm touching that thing – haven't we had enough trauma and supernatural shit over the past year?

CLICK

CLACK

Okay, here goes. Shannon, Brett – something strange is going on around here.

Ummm, Ali, no shit. It's Richland.
Please Ali, let me just have one glass of rosé.

Dad, no! Give me a break. I know you're grieving, and scared - but you have got to keep your shit together.
Ali, what is happening here?
What's going on?

Here's what's going on. Pops – Jared – is here. With us. Dad and I know it. We sense it all the time. I can feel him here right now.
OUIJA
ABCDEFGHIJKLM
NOPQRSTUVWXYZ
1234567890

Ditto. He's here. I can sense him, I can smell him, I know he's here.

Now?
How long has this been going on?
Since the funeral. That's where I – and Dad – first felt it.
And that's not all. We think he's trying to tell us something.

First witches.
Now ghosts?
What's next, vampires?

I would not be surprised, not in this town. Not one bit. Werewolves, zombies, it's an open playing field.
Toxic shit is in the air... witches... crazy people everywhere... God damn potato donuts... assholes... why not ghosts?

Look, I hear you. Sorry Brett, I've never told you this
– but I often think I can feel my uncle in the room with me.

Oh my God, this place. The fun never ends.
This is where I wish I could say let's all drink to that.

Ali, what do you think he's trying to tell you?

Remember that lady I told you about – "Jane" – who told Dad that she knew that tunnel out there was going to collapse?
We've tried to find her, and tried to reach out to his co-workers, his boss... no one will talk to us.

And we have no way of finding out who Jane really is, or how to get a hold of her.
You guys told me about that group – Hanford Connect – Dad and I went to their meeting – we met them.

Apparently there are hundreds of people around here who have gotten sick, made safety complaints, filed claims – and people at Hanford making their lives hell for doing it.
Hanford Connect

That's why we never hear anything about these problems. No one wants to get involved – tell the truth – speak up. They're terrified.

I think Jared wants to help us.
Help us find Jane. Expose those fuckers. To keep this from happening to others.

Jesus Christ. Look, I love having my ghost husband around... but I'm way too jumpy for this shit. Jared, if you are there, cool it with the fucking light flickering.
I'm going to have a heart attack.
CLICK
CLICK

Okay – remember – we got through the Witch curse, and all that – and came out all the better. Shannon, you know this better than anyone. Let's just try this.
Pops kind of gave us a clue that this Ouija Board might be the way to go.
OUIJA

Shannon, it's up to you. I know that you went through a lot, and this kind of shit really freaks you out.

Ali, only because you are the smartest person I know. And Van, because you are the sweetest person I know. Let's give it a go.

Candles, Madame Ali? Really?

Just trust me. You know I've done my research on this.
And we all saw Hereditary.
We need candles.

Oh Christ Ali. We all know how that turned out for that family. The last thing I need is to see my husband crawling along the ceiling like a demon spider.
Though you know I love that Toni Collette.

CLICK

First off, a few ground rules. We must take this seriously. And don't be frightened – we are trying to reach Pops – though there might be other entities out there.

Let's try – and Dad I'm looking at you
– to stay positive about all of this.
Shannon, here's paper and a pen in case we need to take notes.

Okay – everybody put your fingertips on the planchette.

Plan what?
Planchette. The instrument that will help guide us.

Gurl, you know Ali did her Ouija research here. Planchette it up, Cate Planchette.

I'm going to start with an easy one. Hi – Pops – it's Ali. And Van.
And Brett and Shannon. Are you here with us?

Jared, honey, I know you are there. Can you let us know that you are here?

Shannon, I don't want this to freak you out, but I'm going to try something different. In Latin.
Okay Ali, just no scary chanting.
Oh snap, buckle up. Shit's about to get real.
I promise no chanting. Just some simple Latin. Manes proximi, vos evoco.
It's moving! Remember, just barely keep your fingers on it.
W-E-A-R-E-H-E-R-E. What? We are here?

Jesus Ali, how many ghosts did you summon?
Are there more than one of you here with us now?

M-A-N-Y Many. Oh no... I just wanted Pops.
Jesus, we are now surrounded by an army of Hanford ghosts. What did you say exactly?

I guess I summoned all nearby ghosts.

Ummm, Ali – this is Richland. That's summoning a shitload of Hanford ghosts.
They're everywhere around here. Maybe try scaling it down, to Jared?

Okay, okay. Let me think. Okay, let me try this. Manes in domo, accedite.

I-A-M-H-E-R-E.
I am here! Pops, is it just you now? Can you hear me?

Y-E-S. Pops! I –

– we – miss you so much. Please, don't ever leave us.
Jared... my love. I love you so much. And miss you so much. You don't even know.

I'm trying to keep my shit together, but it's, it's hard. And now knowing that this could have been been avoided. Those fuckers out there –

Pops – we want to help you right this wrong that was done to you.

There's one person that we know can help, help us, in proving that the tunnel was doomed – who's Jane? I know her name is not Jane.
Who's the lady you worked with who made complaints about the tunnel not being safe, having cracks... we need to talk to her, but are having no luck locating her.

J-E-N-H-A-R-R-I-S Jen Harris? That's her name, Jen Harris! Dad, how do we find her?

5-0-9 – Shannon, it's a phone number – write this down!

9-4-6-4-3-8-9

Got it. That's her phone number!
Ali, we need to call her, before we have to go back to school. Let's talk to her!

AAAAAH!

Chapter SEVEN

KNOCK
KNOCK
KNOCK

Hi, come in please. And thanks for wearing these -uh - disguises?

Feels a little weird. But thanks for having us over, and hearing us out. We didn't meet at the funeral - I'm Ali.
Jared was my dad. And this is my friend, Shannon.
Nice to meet you.

First off, can I hug you?
I'm so sorry for your loss. Jared was - he was the nicest guy. I miss him so much.

Second off, we have to make this quick. I shouldn't even be talking to you. If anyone sees that you are here, things will get worse for me than they already are.
Excuse me, but what does that mean? Who even knows who we are, and that we would be here?

You girls are young. You don't know what happens around here, when you work – out there – and speak up about anything... what they do to you...
and I think they are already on high alert, with my complaints, Jared's death. I saw a few of them at your dad's funeral.

Are you serious? Doing what?

I'm sure just scoping it out. Making sure no one is trying to expose anything.
There's big money involved out there, and they have people full-time just spying around here.

This is surreal. Do you think they are watching us now?

Get away from that window! I wouldn't be surprised.

You told my Dad at the funeral that you were with my Pops – Jared – when that tunnel collapsed?
Can you tell us anything about it?

Do you girls mind if I smoke?
No, it's your house. Go ahead.

Okay, here's the deal. I've worked out there for years. Field work.
I've seen what happens when anyone questions anything out there.
But I saw that tunnel collapse coming for months.
There were cracks – they just kept getting bigger – and yet they still wanted us to keep working out there.
Oh, I pointed out the cracks – took pictures – made a safety report. They shut me down – told me that it was safe – that the cracks had been there for years, and nothing was going to happen.
They even threw some fucking grout on parts of it to try and cover it up. Then that day came... it was awful. Luckily we all got out alive.
Your dad – Jared – we were worried he was killed in the collapse. He was the last to come out. And then he pulled his mask off – he should never have done that.
I'm sure that's where it went downhill for him. I'm sorry to talk like this to you, but you should know the truth.
He got sick pretty quickly. I know he filed reports, went to the doctor several times – but they always denied his claims.
That's the standard M.O. out there – deny all claims, until a lawsuit is filed. You know he's not the only one who got sick that day, right?
What?
Who?
You?

Not me, I'm okay. Just some dizzy spells, night sweats. But I'm getting by.
No, there were four of us there that day. Myself, your dad, and two others.

One of them is really sick – in the hospital. Phil. Phil Thompson.

Like your dad, he started feeling shitty not long after the tunnel collapsed –
Cough Cough
no wonder, with all of those hidden tanks of millions of gallons of toxic shit down there.

Hanford denied his claims as well.
He hasn't developed full blown cancer, like your dad did – but he's really fucked up. Can hardly breathe without a tube.

What about your reports? Did anything ever come of them?

I brought it up a few more times, after the incident. Do you know what those pricks did to me after that?
They made me go see a psychiatrist. Like I was crazy.

They also demoted me, put me on a desk job. Less pay. Less hours.
And no one will speak to me. They call me a snitch behind my back, under their breath. I went to HR, filed a report. That was a few months ago – nothing ever came of it –

– other than the fact that I know I'm being watched. There's a van out there all the time – it's not there now, thankfully.
And my phone is tapped, I know it. That's why I use a burner phone now. How'd you get this number anyways? I didn't give it to anyone...

It's complicated. I can't tell you that. But I can give you my word it wasn't from anyone at Hanford.
Hey – have you reached out to a lawyer – or have you had any contact with Hanford Connect? They protect people like you.

Look, I need my job. I need my benefits. I'm sure I'll be getting sick one of these days – I worked out there for so many years.
And just before the tunnel, they had us at the tank farms – and – not sure if you've heard the secret tagline for the tank farms –

One sniff, you're stiff.
And I had many sniffs. So I just want to stay under the radar here, collect my check and my benefits, and carry on. I'm a single mom with a daughter in college.
And I know about Hanford Connect – we've all heard stories of what happens if you contact them – sure, I know they've settled many cases –
namely working with the Downwinders – but just me making that call will put me in the hotseat.

I can't deal with that now. I tried to stop anyone from getting hurt in that tunnel collapse, and it went nowhere.

Ms. Harris – Jen – I really appreciate you talking with us. And I can't make you do anything you don't want to do.
But I do have a favor to ask – I can't let my dad's death go unnoticed, with no one held accountable.

I'm begging you – can you just get me a copy of the complaints you filed about the tunnel? That's it.

That report would be enough for us to at least show that they should have known, should have stopped it.
And my other Dad is about to lose his shit again, go off the rails – he needs closure. And this would do it.

Well, that would get me fired for sure. They would obviously know it came from me. There's no way – I'm so sorry – but I can't help you.
Besides, I don't have them – I filled out the complaint forms, and turned them in right there in the office. I'm sorry, but I can't help.

Well fuck. I have to ask. If there's any way you'd talk to someone – at Hanford Connect. They've been so great, and all they want to do is help people who are exactly in your shoes – and my family's shoes!

Please Jen...come with us. We can all go in disguise. Obs we've got that part mastered.

CRASH
AAAAAAAHH
AAAHHH

Oh Christ, they know. They know. I'm cooked. You girls – you have to leave. I'm sorry I can't help.
Please, leave now – put your hoodies up – and sneak out the back door. This way.

I'm so sorry this is happening to you. It's such bullshit. You have my number – if you change your mind, call me. Please.
Any time. They could help you get a settlement as well, for retaliation – you could start over.

LOCK

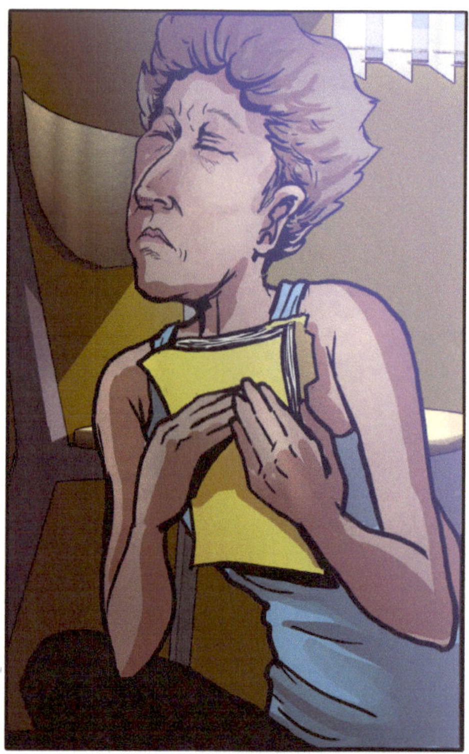

PLOCK

HOSPITAL
Chapter EIGHT

EMERGENCY
AMBULANCE

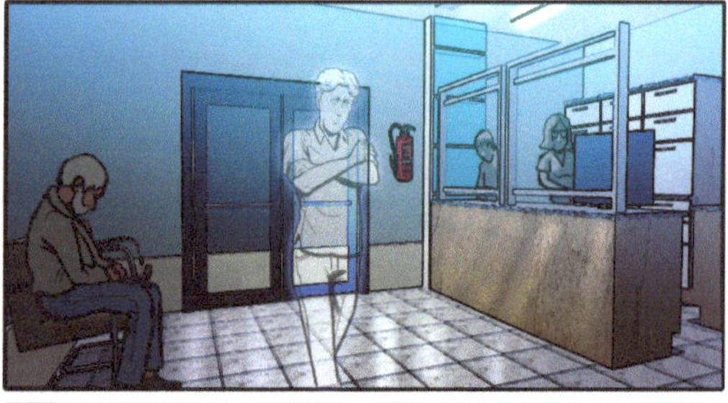

I'm sure you have questions. Many. I do as well. I know that I'm no longer alive.

I know that I am surrounded by many others just like me – many who perished in similar ways – by this town – this haunted and toxic town.

This place... out there... built for destruction, to kill others, and killing many of its own denizens.

Built that deadly bomb, killing so many people. A true dead zone – nine weapons reactors, 177 underground tanks full of deadly waste.
That place – that place that produced 74 tons of plutonium.

Those tanks – those fucking tanks, with 56 million gallons of radioactive waste buried in this town's precious soil.

Spills into that river that everyone loves. Vapors emanating from the ground. And yet everyone around here seems to ignore it, ignore the danger, the reality.
The companies, the contractors, the subcontractors – the fucking government – deny the truth, deny the danger, and ignore the signs.

They ignore the thousands plagued with health issues – the cancer – thyroid disorders – handicaps of all types – because the river, the dirt, the air, the pollution.
Even toxic tumbleweeds blowing around town.

They ignore it when someone dies... though millions have been exposed to this radiation.

So, here I am. So here – we are –

And here they are – the ones we love – the ones left behind.

We try to help them – reach them – touch them.
HOSPITAL

I could at first – we all could – but that ability seems to be fading away. I don't think I have much time before I'll be out of their lives forever.
But until that time... I'll do what I am still able to do...

Jared? Jared is that you? Ali, he's here, he's here with us now.

Pops! Pops I feel you. Any help you can give us today, please... I know you're here with us.

Come on Dad. Let's see this through.

This feels so weird. Like we are rogue spies or something. Like we are in Get Smart.
That's the most recent spy reference you have? Sad. Come on, follow me... and for God's sake don't make a fool of yourself. I'm pretty certain that he will be under some sort of covert surveillance or something.

Luckily Jen told us his room number. This is it. Let's go.

Phil? Phil Thompson? Are you awake?

Who are you?

I'm Ali – Ali Fleming. And this is Van Fleming. Jared Fleming was my dad –
And my husband. Phil, we are so so sorry that you are in here, dealing with this. Do you mind if we ask you a few questions?

We probably don't have long. There's usually someone sitting out there, watching – you know – from Hanford...
And I'm really sorry about Jared. He was so nice. Really sorry for your loss.

I'm here now. Just grabbed a coffee. It's been quiet today – some family stopped by, nothing to report about. No, no one else. I'll stay at least until visiting hours end.

Thank you. Look, we won't be long.
You should be resting, and this seems like maybe our only chance.

Excuse me, who are you? You can't be in –

SLAM
LOCK

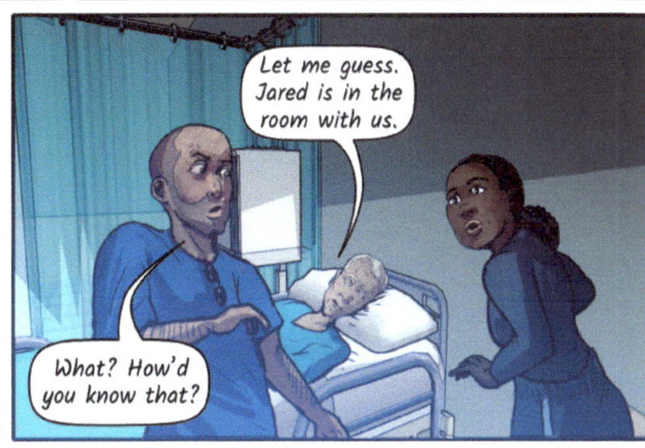
Let me guess. Jared is in the room with us.
What? How'd you know that?

I've been here for a few weeks now. This place is full of ghosts, or spirits, or whatever they are.
Angels?
I feel them all around me.

I think they come see me because they died out there... and maybe they want to help me?
Feel sorry for me maybe. I'm not sure.
Well shit. This town gets more fucked by the day.

HAHA
COUGH
COUGH
Ah fuck. Sorry. Please, don't laugh. Ali, you do the talking. I'll do the recording.

Recording?

Phil, I know you were there. We just want to hear from you on that experience, and the time leading up to it.
We want to prove that those fuckers should have known, and stopped the work from happening out there. But no one will talk to us, no one will help us.

I'm hoping that you can. Please please please – for my Pops, Jared – and for others around here who've gotten sick, even died, out there – or just tried to step up and speak up on what's happening out there, and reporting safety violations, all that –

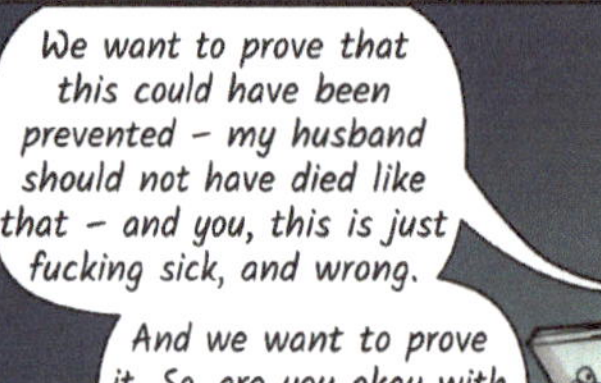
We want to prove that this could have been prevented – my husband should not have died like that – and you, this is just fucking sick, and wrong.
And we want to prove it. So, are you okay with that? We probably only have a few minutes before that fucker out there –

BANG
BANG
BANG

Well fuck it. Go for it. I'll tell you what I know.
Great. Can you state your name, and today's date?

Phil Thompson. This is... shit, what is today?
I think it's Saturday, April 20th.
Phil, were you working at the tunnel near the Hanford B Reactor on the day of the collapse, back in October of last year, along with my father, Jared Fleming?

I was. Yes, I was.

How long after that tunnel collapse did you start getting sick?
COUGH
HMPH
COUGH

It was about a few days later. I couldn't breathe right, was getting dizzy. Really dizzy. And I couldn't really focus.

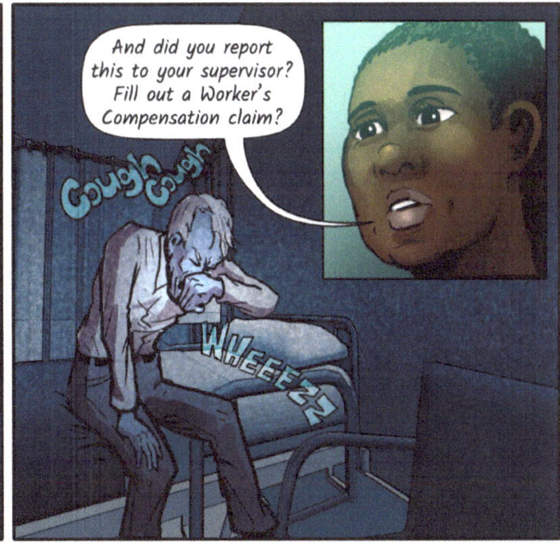
And did you report this to your supervisor? Fill out a Worker's Compensation claim?
Cough Cough
WHEEEEZZ

I did. Yes, I did. Pricks, they of course declined it. Said whatever was wrong with me, that it had nothing to do with the tunnel. Or radiation.
Or Hanford.
Were you able to appeal it?

I started that process. But it's worthless. Everybody tells me that. Don't bother. Then I just got sicker, and kind of dropped it.

Were you aware of the cracks in that tunnel before the collapse? Had you seen them before?
EXIT

Fuck yeah. We all did. Maybe not your pop – he was the new guy. But yeah, we all saw it. Reported it.
I know that at least one of my co-workers filed a formal report to the Safety Department. They ignored her.

Jen? Was that Jen?
Yes, that was Jen. Bless her heart. She tried.
Then this shit happened, and now look at me. But it's been happening for decades, so why would my case be any different?

Phil, have you been to a lawyer? Contacted Hanford Connect?
I had one meeting with my attorney. And after that, they started following me.

I know that my phone has been tapped – they don't even try to hide that. You know they don't want me talking to anyone. The lawyer is trying to work on it, but I know he's getting stonewalled. I doubt that will go anywhere.

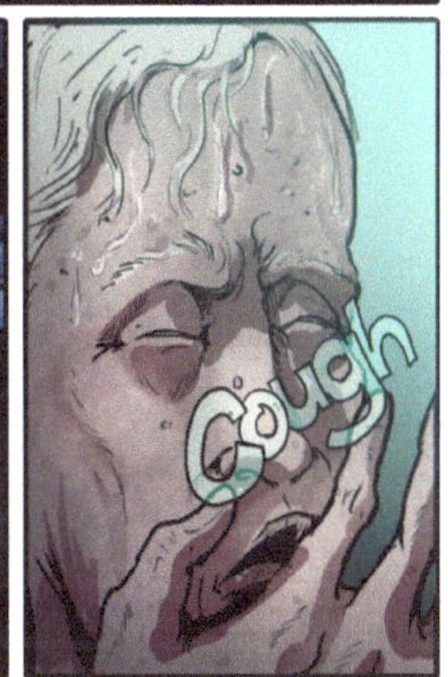
Cough

SKRAT
Well, at least someone is on our side.

We better go. Phil, this has been so helpful.
Maybe it will help your case also...

You people need to leave now. You should not be here. Did you record him? Give me your phone –

Fuck you. Are you threatening us? Who even are you, fuckity fuckface.

You guys should go. Thanks for coming. Good luck.

What the fuck? Who's there?

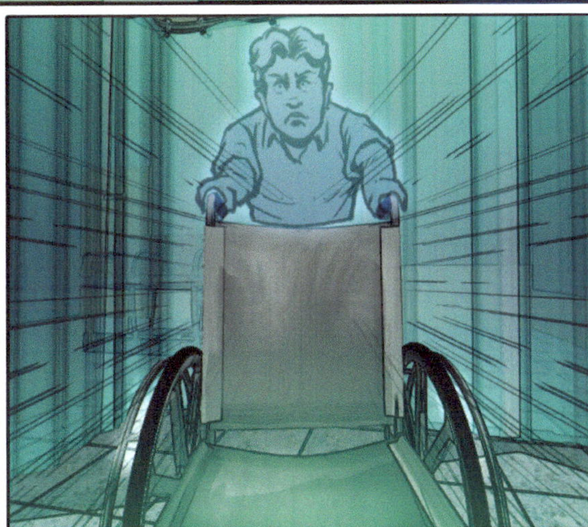

Now you get the fuck away from me. You're not on my visitor list. FUCK YOU!

Chapter NINE

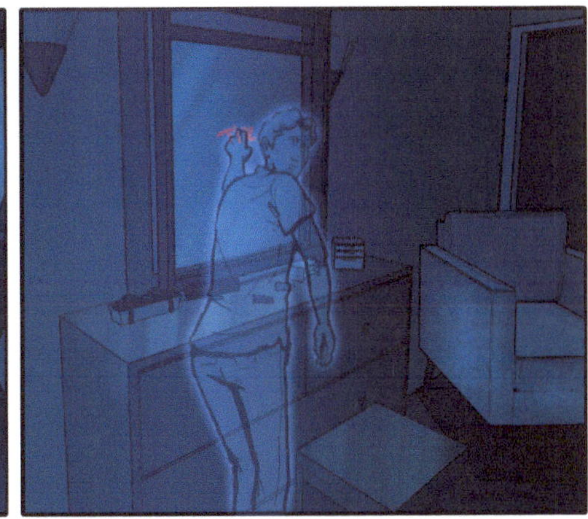

They're
here

They're
here

Get the fuck out of my house.

Hold on now.. no need for –

BANG

Leave now, or I'll blow your fucking brains out.

Thank you, whoever's there.
LOCK

I need to report a burglary, at my house. Please send help, now!

Chapter TEN

HOSPITAL

PITAL

Excuse me, nurse?

Hi – where's the patient who's been in this room? Phil Thompson?

Ma'am, I'm so sorry. He passed away last night. Are you family?

Oh, no, just a close friend. Thank you.

Phil? Is that you?

Uh, hi. It's me, Jen. I need to see you now.
I have something for you.
Yes, it's time.

Exit

Chapter ELEVEN

Welcome
Hanford Connect
Attendees

Welcome
Hanford Connect
Attendees

Hi everyone. Yes, I'm still around, I guess this is my existence now – I will always be around here, in this town that killed me, walking amongst all of my new –

- friends.

Most of whom – of which there are many of us – have also been wronged by this place.

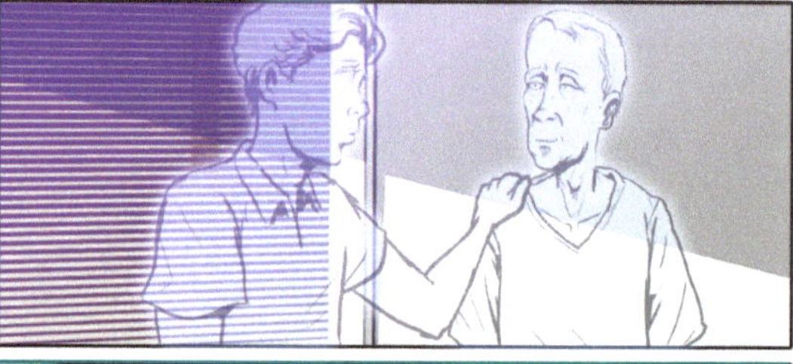

So many people have been wronged here – I've met – I'll say entities – like myself, who've perished in this town, in the same local hospital...

...mostly buried at the same local graveyard – going back many many decades.

Babies, kids, young adults, and seniors. Many are angry.
Many – like myself – now resolved, and just simply – co-existing.

Angry or upset as we are, in this state – there's only so much we can do.
After time, our ability to make contact with those living diminishes – even on the Ouija Board!

Since we last spoke, some time has gone by. I'm not sure anymore. But I know much has happened. Things have been resolved – at least with my family.

And her – that lovely woman who risked the danger and decided to take a stand.

A stand that worked – she no longer has to live like that – in fact it appears that she is moving away from here.

And these two – the loves of my life – are doing the same. There's no reason for them to stay.
They need to move on, enjoy their lives. I will always be watching them.

One day Van will join me – one day Ali will join us. Until that time though...

My friends, let's get started. Welcome to the regular meeting of Hanford Connect. We have some new faces – welcome – and most of you, I know, are regular or returning friends.

I always like to start with the good news – settlements, and resolutions. We have had a run of success recently, settling several issues – some surrounding the tunnel collapse of nearly two years ago.

For those of you in the room today – I won't single you out –

But I want to thank you for your patience, and also doggedness and determination, in this case.
There's only so much hiding of the truth that can happen, and you worked diligently with us at Hanford Connect to right those wrong –

– and hopefully quell future wrongdoings, and accidents – because believe you me, there will be more – hell, we've had at least a dozen cases in the past few weeks –

Look – there are 177 tanks buried in the ground there, full of that toxic shit.

And those tanks are leaking.
And there will be more leaks, and more malfunctions, and people breathing in that dust and working around those tanks.

And they will get sick. And when they do, we will be there to help however we can.

And looking around this room – you all – you all who have taken the risk, brought issues to the light, and safety concerns to management – you are the true heroes –

– the whistleblowers of Hanford, of Richland – let's call it Snitchland –
you strive to bring to light the lies, the escaping of liability, and also the tactics used to try to silence you from seeking truth, and seeking justice.

So thank you, all of you.

This has to change. This has to stop. They need to figure out how to clean this shit up, safely.

And thank you to those who started this movement before us – the Downwinders – who unfortunately were just trying to live – to farm, to raise families, to make a living – and through no fault of their own, were subjected to all of those releases of airborne radiation.

I digress. And will get off my soap box.
Now, on to new business. As for new cases, we have a few. Mostly related to the digging out at the tank farms.

We have three reports of phone tampering, two reported cases of home break-ins, and three cases of...

Chapter TWELVE

FOR SALE

Do you remember Ali, just a few years ago we were unpacking our things from Seattle at our little Hanford government home – I hated that place.
Don't remind me of that shit show of a house. And let's not talk about a certain neighbor of ours, she whom we won't name, or her fucking witch sticks.

He tried. Jared really tried. He knew we didn't want to leave Seattle, and move here – but he did it for us.
For you, and your college future. He really was trying to make a better life for us. And look how all of that ended up.

Look – I'm still worried about you. Are you sure you're going to be all right on your own?
I don't mind taking a year of college off, to be with you, help you get settled in your new place.

Don't talk that bullshit Ali – you need to get back to school, finish that degree. I'm counting on you to take care of me in my old age.
And you only have one more year of school! I'll be fine.

I know he's still here, with us. Though I can't physically feel him, I know he's still here. I hope this feeling never goes away.

Oh honey, I know he's here. He'll always be here. Look, he always urged us to be – what's that fucking phrase – trail blazers. Ali, go blaze a trail. If any one could, it would be you.

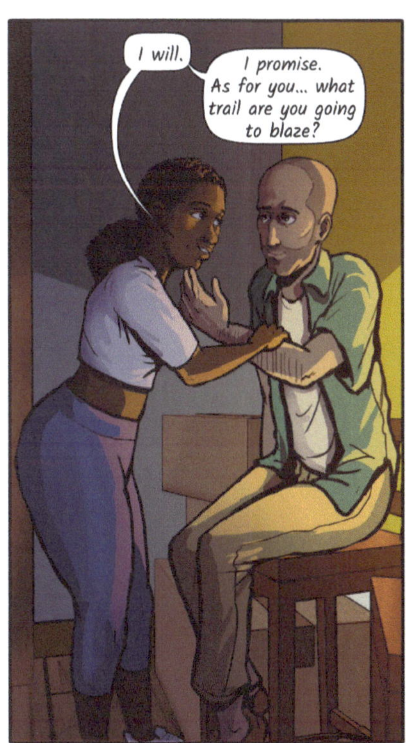
I will.
I promise. As for you... what trail are you going to blaze?

I'm not sure. But maybe this is my time to find something that I love to do. And that starts with me getting out of this town for good.

CLICK
AHH!

God dammit Jared!

Meanwhile...somewhere else in Snitchland...
I shouldn't be telling you this. They could be listening. Yes, I filed that complaint. And oh, get this – I got sent to the company psychiatrist.
They are making me out like I'm a crazy person.

No, they didn't do anything about it. I'm not sure what I expected, but it certainly wasn't this.
My career out here is now over, just because I spoke up and told the truth.

TICK TICK TICK TICK

Wait, what was that. Did you hear a click?

Hello, who's there? Who's listening in?

Hello? Who is this?

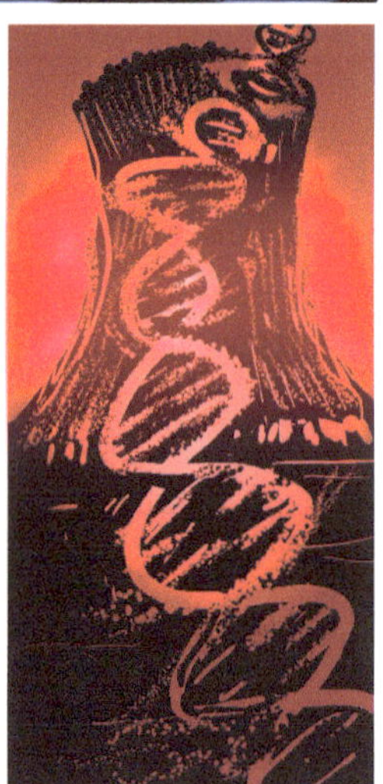

Epilogue

ATOMIC
PIZZA

ATOMIC
PIZZA

ATOMIC
RING
RING
RING

ATOMIC
PIZZA
Oh, hey Van. Yup, got the pizza. I hope you got me a beer or two.
I'll be over in a few.

SQUEAK
EEEK
SQUEAK
EEEK
Wait, what the...
ATOMIC
PIZZA

EEEK
SQUEAK
Jesus fuck. Bats? What the hell is going...
SQUEAK
EEEK

ATOMIC PIZZA
ATOMIC
EEEK
SQUEAK
EEEK
SQUEAK
AGHHHHHH

Brett? What's going on? Brett?

Brett, are you okay?

ATOMIC PIZZA
Hey, yeah. Sorry about that Van. I'll be right over.
THE END

www.ingramcontent.com/pod-product-compliance
Lightning Source LLC
Chambersburg PA
CBHW040823050726
47507CB00021B/107

* 9 7 9 8 9 9 0 8 4 8 8 0 1 *